# FOREWORD

*The Kissing Hand* is a story for any child who confronts a difficult situation, and for the child within each of us who sometimes needs reassurance. Its gentle text and vibrant illustrations reminded me of the classic children's books I enjoyed with my own children, and left me with the warm, wonderful feeling that is the test of a true children's classic.

Even before this book was considered for publication by the Child Welfare League of America, Audrey Penn had presented her story to children in schools, libraries, and children's hospitals. I'm delighted that now it can reach a wider audience and enable people to face many kinds of challenges with the confidence to cope.

A child entering a new school or going away to camp, a child entering foster care or residential care, a child facing a temporary separation from loved ones or the death of a parent, grandparent, or other special person, even a fearful adult, will find reassurance in these pages. Parents and others who care for children will find an unforgettable way of communicating the message that all of us most need to hear—"You are loved."

*Jean Kennedy Smith*
*Founder and Program Chairperson*
*Very Special Arts*
*Washington, DC*

# The
# KISSING HAND

## by Audrey Penn
### Illustrated by Ruth E. Harper and Nancy M. Leak

Tanglewood · Indianapolis

Published by Tanglewood Publishing, Inc., 2006.
© 1993 Audrey Penn

TANGLEWOOD PUBLISHING, INC.
1060 N. Capitol Ave., Ste. E-395, Indianapolis, IN 46204, www.tanglewoodbooks.com

Cover Design by Andrew Arnold. Book design by S. Dmitri Lipczenko and Typography by Hannah Kleber, Rockville, MD
Manufactured by LSC in the United States of America.
10 9 8 7

ISBN-13 978-1-939100-42-9

*Library of Congress Cataloging-in-Publication Data*
Penn, Audrey, 1947-
   The Kissing Hand / Audrey Penn; illustrations by Ruth E. Harper and Nancy M. Leak.
      p. cm.
   Summary: When Chester the raccoon is reluctant to go to kindergarten for the first time, his
mother teaches him a secret way to carry her love with him.
   ISBN 1-933718-00-5 (alk. paper)
 [1. Separation anxiety-Fiction. 2. Mothers and sons-Fiction. 3. Raccoons-Fiction. 4. Forest animals-Fiction.
5. Kindergarten-Fiction. 6. Schools-Fiction.]  I. Harper, Ruth E., ill. II. Leak, Nancy M., ill. III. Title.
   PZ7.P38448Ki 2006
   [Fic]-dc22
                                             2006003727

To: Stefanie Rebecca Koren
and children everywhere
who love to be loved.

Chester Raccoon stood at the edge of the forest and cried.

"I don't want to go to school," he told his mother. "I want to stay home with you. I want to play with my friends. And play with my toys. And read my books. And swing on my swing. Please may I stay home with you?"

Mrs. Raccoon took Chester by the hand and nuzzled him on the ear.

"Sometimes we all have to do things we don't want to do," she told him gently. "Even if they seem strange and scary at first. But you will love school once you start."

"You'll make new friends. And play with new toys."

"Read new books. And swing on new swings. Besides," she added. "I know a wonderful secret that will make your nights at school seem as warm and cozy as your days at home."

Chester wiped away his tears and looked interested. "A secret? What kind of secret?"

"A very old secret," said Mrs. Raccoon. "I learned it from my mother, and she  learned it from hers. It's called the Kissing Hand."

"The Kissing Hand?" asked Chester. "What's that?"

"I'll show you." Mrs. Raccoon took Chester's left hand and spread open his tiny fingers into a fan. Leaning forward, she kissed Chester right in the middle of his palm.

Chester felt his mother's kiss rush from his hand, up his arm, and into his heart. Even his silky, black mask tingled with a special warmth.

Mrs. Raccoon smiled. "Now," she told Chester, "whenever you feel lonely and need a little loving from home, just press your hand to your cheek and think, 'Mommy loves you. Mommy loves you.' And that very kiss will jump to your face and fill you with toasty warm thoughts."

She took Chester's hand and carefully wrapped his fingers around the kiss. "Now, do be careful not to lose it," she teased him. "But, don't worry. When you open your hand and wash your food, I promise the kiss will stick."

Chester loved his Kissing Hand. Now he knew
his mother's love would go with him wherever he went.
Even to school.

That night, Chester stood in front of his school and looked thoughtful. Suddenly, he turned to his mother and grinned.

"Give me your hand," he told her.

Chester took his mother's hand
in his own and unfolded her large, familiar
fingers into a fan. Next, he leaned forward
and kissed the center of her hand.

"Now you have a Kissing Hand, too,"
he told her. And with a gentle "Good-bye" and
"I love you," Chester turned and danced away.

Mrs. Raccoon watched Chester scamper across a tree limb and enter school. And as the hoot owl rang in the new school year, she pressed her left hand to her cheek and smiled.

The warmth of Chester's kiss filled her heart with special words.

"Chester loves you," it sang. "Chester loves you."

I LOVE YOU